Owlkids Books Inc.
10 Lower Spadina Avenue, Suite 400, Toronto, Ontario M5V 2Z2
www.owlkids.com

North America edition © 2011 Owlkids Books Inc.

Text and Illustrations © 2009 Paloma Valdivia
Translation © 2011 Susan Ouriou

Published in Spain under the title *Los de arriba y los de abajo* © 2010
Kalandraka Ediciones Andalucía
www.kalandraka.com

Distributed in Canada by University of Toronto Press
5201 Dufferin Street, Toronto, Ontario M3H 5T8

Distributed in the United States by Publishers Group West
1700 Fourth Street, Berkeley, California 94710

Library and Archives Canada Cataloguing in Publication

Valdivia, Paloma
    Up above and down below / Paloma Valdivia.

Translation of: Los de arriba y los de abajo.
ISBN 978-1-926973-39-5

    I. Title.

PZ7.V253Up 2012   j863'.7   C2011-907564-4

Library of Congress Control Number: 2011943194

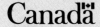

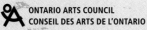

We acknowledge the financial support of the Canada Council for the Arts, the Ontario Arts Council, the
Government of Canada through the Canada Book Fund (CBF) and the Government of Ontario through
the Ontario Media Development Corporation's Book Initiative for our publishing activities.

Manufactured by C&C Joint Printing Co., (Guangdong) Ltd.
Manufactured in Shenzhen, China, in December 2011
Job #201111609

A   B   C   D   E   F

Publisher of Chirp, chickaDEE and OWL
www.owlkids.com

For Aunt Margarita,
who used to live
down below but now
does her sewing up above

For Michael Nyman
(this story comes
with its own soundtrack)

Up Above and Down Below

By Paloma Valdivia

In the world, there are different kinds of people.

Some live up above and some live down below.

The ones up above live just like the ones down below.

And the ones down below live just like the ones up above,
only the other way around.

On the top, they think the ones on the bottom are different.

On the bottom, they think the ones on the top are different.

But they're all the same, except in a few small ways.

When the ones up above put on their bathing suits,
the ones down below open up their umbrellas.

When spring makes its entrance in one place,
fall pushes its way into the other.

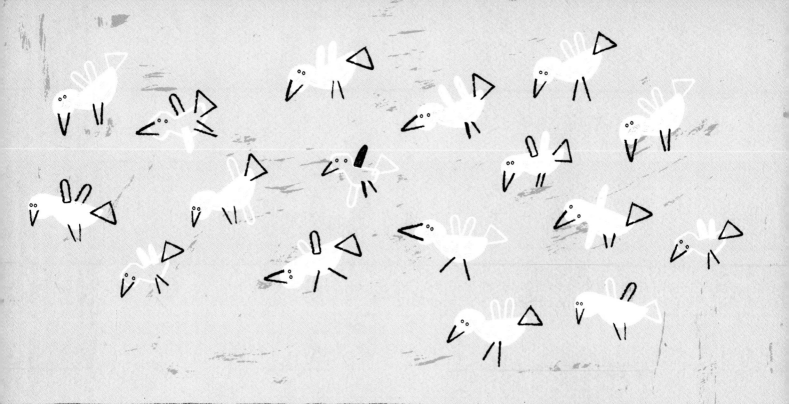

If it's planting time up above, it's harvest time down below.

The ones up above go down.

The ones down below go up.

Now and then, they all dream of flying. But, then...

...who is from up above and who is from down below?

They can all look at the world the other way around.

They can all look at the world the other way around.

Map of Up Above and Down Below